MARC BROWN

Queen for a Day

QUEEN of
ELWOOD CITY

The Mayor was about to announce the winner
of an essay contest at Arthur's school.

Everyone held their breath. Muffy really wanted to win. The winner was going to ride in the "City Pride" Parade as King or Queen of Elwood City.

"And the winner is…" Mr. Haney began, "Muffy Crosswire!"

"What a surprise!" Muffy cried.

"Smile, Muffy," called Buster's mom, snapping her picture.

After school, Muffy gathered everyone together.

"I have to plan my float for the parade," she announced, "and choose who will perform with me. Be prepared with your talent presentations on Saturday. We'll meet at my house."

"Oh, this is so exciting," Francine said. "Maybe I could perform a…"

"Francine," Muffy interrupted, "as my best friend, I think you should sing this song I wrote. It's a tribute to me."

On Saturday, Prunella came dressed in a long gown. "I designed this myself," she explained. "Rubella helped me make it. What do you think?"

"Not bad," said Muffy. "You will be my Lady-in-Waiting. Who's next?"

Binky Barnes got up to juggle. "You're in," Muffy said, checking off his name.

After Binky, Buster told some jokes. Muffy rolled her eyes.
"You will be my Master of Ceremonies," said Muffy. "But no jokes."

Fern read a poem.

"Very nice, Fern," Muffy began. "You may write a poem in honor of me to read aloud on the float. And Arthur will accompany you on the piano."

"I have a design for your float," said the Brain.

"I want it to raise up and turn around slowly, so I can wave to all my fans equally," said Muffy.

"Did it," said the Brain. "It has a sophisticated hydraulic lift with a turning radius of 360 degrees."

"Francine, did you learn the song I gave you?" asked Muffy.

"Well," Francine explained nervously. "I tried to, but…"

"You may begin!" Muffy insisted.

Francine cleared her throat and sang a few notes.

"Stop!" Muffy cried. "That sounds awful, Francine!
If you can't sing, you can't ride on the float."

Francine felt terrible. "I'm leaving!" she cried.

"Wait!" Arthur called. "Don't go!"

"I don't want to ride on her crummy float!" said Francine.

After she left, Arthur spoke to Muffy. "Francine isn't coming back. Maybe you could apologize."

"Francine is just too sensitive," Muffy snapped.

When they left Muffy's house, Arthur turned to his friends. "We have to do something," he insisted.

"Muffy is out of control," Buster added.

"Yeah!" Binky agreed.

"If Muffy thinks she's so special, then she can ride on the float all by herself," said Arthur.

The next day, when Muffy called her first rehearsal,
no one showed up.

"Fine!" exclaimed Muffy. "I don't need any of you!
I can do it all myself!"

Muffy went to her father. "Daddy," she said, "I want you to hire a crew to operate my float and find me some professional entertainers."

"Calm down, Cupcake," said Mr. Crosswire. "I'll take care of everything."

Mr. Crosswire met with the parade people. Everything that Muffy wanted was against the rules. Muffy was very disappointed. She didn't really want to ride on the float by herself.

Secret Clubhouse

Muffy went to see Arthur.

"If you want our help, you need to be a lot nicer to everybody," Arthur explained. "And let Francine ride with you."

"But she can't sing," Muffy insisted.

"Everyone is good at different things," said Arthur. "Just think of something else for Francine to do."

Muffy thought for a moment. She pictured herself all alone on an empty float.

"Okay," Muffy agreed grudgingly. "I'll try."

As Muffy was leaving, she saw D.W. playing with her baton in the driveway.

"If only Francine could twirl like you," Muffy said.

"Francine's the one who taught me how," said D.W. "Hey, Muffy, watch this!" D.W. threw the baton way up in the air and caught it.

"Great!" exclaimed Muffy. "I've got to find Francine."

Muffy saw Francine coming out of the Sugar Bowl.

"What do you want?" Francine asked.

Muffy used her sweetest voice. "I thought of something fabulous you can do on the float."

"You can twirl the baton," said Muffy

"Okay," Francine agreed. "I love to twirl!"

"Just one thing..." said Muffy.

"What's the matter now?" asked Francine

"You get to twirl on the royal float," Muffy said,
"but no singing!"